He wanted to show that fate ruled people's lives,

and that those who interfered with it did so to their sorrow.

CREATIVE SHORT STORIES

THE MONKEY'S PAW

W. W. JACOBS

CREATIVE EDUCATION

Without, the night was cold and wet, but in the small parlor of Lakesnam Villa the blinds were drawn and the fire burned brightly. Father and son were at chess, the former, who possessed ideas about the game involving radical changes, putting his king into such sharp and unnecessary perils that it even provoked comment from the white-haired old lady knitting placidly by the fire.

"Hark at the wind," said Mr. White, who, having seen a fatal mistake after it was too late, was amiably desirous of preventing his son from seeing it.

"I'm listening," said the latter, grimly surveying the board as he stretched out his hand. "Check."

"I should hardly think that he'd come tonight," said his father, with his hand poised over the board.

"Mate," replied the son.

"That's the worst of living so far out," bawled Mr. White, with sudden and unlooked-for violence; "of all the beastly, slushy, out-of-the-way places to live in, this is the worst. Pathway's a bog, and the road's a torrent. I don't know what people are thinking about. I suppose because only two houses on the road are let, they think it doesn't matter."

"Never mind, dear," said his wife soothingly; "perhaps you'll win

the next one."

Mr. White looked up sharply, just in time to intercept a knowing glance between mother and son. The words died away on his lips, and he hid a guilty grin in his thin gray beard.

"There he is," said Herbert White, as the gate banged to loudly and heavy footsteps came toward the door.

The old man rose with hospitable haste, and opening the door, was heard condoling with the new arrival. The new arrival also condoled with himself, so that Mrs. White said, "Tut, tut!" and coughed gently as her husband entered the room, followed by a tall burly man, beady of eye and rubicund of visage.

"Sergeant Major Morris," he said, introducing him.

The sergeant major shook hands, and taking the proffered seat by the fire, watched contentedly while his host got out whiskey and tumblers and stood a small copper kettle on the fire.

At the third glass his eyes got brighter, and he began to talk, the little family circle regarding with eager interest this visitor from distant parts, as he squared his broad shoulders in the chair and spoke of strange scenes and doughty deeds, of wars and plagues and strange peoples.

"Twenty-one years of it," said Mr. White, nodding at his wife and son. "When he went away he was a slip of a youth in the warehouse. Now look at him."

"He don't look to have taken much harm," said Mrs. White politely.

"I'd like to go to India myself," said the old man, "just to look round a bit, you know."

"Better where you are," said the sergeant major, shaking his head. He put down the empty glass and, sighing softly, shook it again.

"I should like to see those old temples and fakirs and jugglers," said the old man. "What was that you started telling me the other day about a monkey's paw or something, Morris?"

"Nothing," said the soldier hastily. "Leastways, nothing worth hearing."

"Monkey's paw?" said Mrs. White curiously.

"Well, it's just a bit of what you might call magic, perhaps," said the sergeant major offhandedly.

His three listeners leaned forward eagerly. The visitor absent-mindedly put his empty glass to his lips and then set it down again. His host filled it for him.

"To look at," said the sergeant major, fumbling in his pocket, "it's just an ordinary little paw, dried to a mummy."

He took something out of his pocket and proffered it. Mrs. White drew back with a grimace, but her son, taking it, examined it curiously.

"And what is there special about it?" inquired Mr. White, as he took it from his son and, having examined it, placed it upon the table.

"It had a spell put on it by an old fakir," said the sergeant major, "a very holy man. He wanted to show that fate ruled people's lives, and that those who interfered with it did so to their sorrow. He put a spell on it so that three separate men could each have three wishes from it."

His manner was so impressive that his hearers were conscious that their light laughter jarred somewhat.

"Well, why don't you have three, sir?" said Herbert White cleverly.

The soldier regarded him in the way that middle age is wont to regard presumptuous youth. "I have," he said quietly, and his blotchy face whitened.

"And did you really have the three wishes granted?" asked Mrs.

White.

"I did," said the sergeant major, and his glass tapped against his strong teeth.

"And has anybody else wished?" inquired the old lady.

"The first man had his three wishes, yes," was the reply. "I don't know what the first two were, but the third was for death. That's how I got the paw."

His tones were so grave that a hush fell upon the group.

"If you've had your three wishes, it's no good to you now, then, Morris," said the old man at last. "What do you keep it for?"

The soldier shook his head. "Fancy, I suppose," he said slowly. "I did have some idea of selling it, but I don't think I will. It has caused enough mischief already. Besides, people won't buy. They think it's a fairy tale, some of them, and those who do think anything of it want to try it first and pay me afterward."

"If you could have another three wishes," said the old man, eyeing him keenly, "would you have them?"

"I don't know," said the other. "I don't know."

He took the paw, and dangling it between his front finger and thumb, suddenly threw it upon the fire. White, with a slight cry, stooped down and snatched it off.

"Better let it burn," said the soldier solemnly.

"If you don't want it, Morris," said the old man, "give it to me."

"I won't," said his friend doggedly. "I threw it on the fire. If you keep it, don't blame me for what happens. Pitch it on the fire again, like a sensible man."

The other shook his head and examined his new possession closely. "How do you do it?" he inquired.

"Hold it up in your right hand and wish aloud," said the sergeant major, "but I warn you of the consequences."

"Sounds like the *Arabian Nights*," said Mrs. White, as she rose and began to set the supper. "Don't you think you might wish for four pairs of hands for me?"

Her husband drew the talisman from his pocket and then all three burst into laughter as the sergeant major, with a look of alarm on his face, caught him by the arm.

"If you must wish," he said gruffly, "wish for something sensible."

Mr. White dropped it back into his pocket, and placing chairs, motioned his friend to the table. In the business of supper the talisman was partly forgotten, and afterward the three sat listening in an enthralled fashion to a second installment of the soldier's adventures in India.

"If the tale about the monkey's paw is not more truthful than those he has been telling us," said Herbert, as the door closed behind their guest, just in time for him to catch the last train, "we shan't make much out of it."

"Did you give him anything for it, Father?" inquired Mrs. White, regarding her husband closely.

"A trifle," said he, coloring slightly. "He didn't want it, but I made him take it. And he pressed me again to throw it away."

"Likely," said Herbert, with pretended horror. "Why, we're going to be rich, and famous, and happy. Wish to be an emperor, Father, to begin with; then you can't be henpecked."

He darted around the table, pursued by the maligned Mrs. White armed with an antimacassar.

Mr. White took the paw from his pocket and eyed it dubiously. "I don't know what to wish for, and that's a fact," he said slowly. "It seems to me I've got all I want."

"If you only cleared the house, you'd be quite happy, wouldn't you?" said Herbert, with his hand on his shoulder. "Well, wish for two hundred pounds, then; that'll just do it."

His father, smiling shamefacedly at his own credulity, held up the talisman, as his son, with a solemn face somewhat marred by a wink at his mother, sat down at the piano and struck a few impressive chords.

"I wish for two hundred pounds," said the old man distinctly.

A fine crash from the piano greeted the words, interrupted by a shuddering cry from the old man. His wife and son ran toward him.

"It moved," he cried, with a glance of disgust at the object as it lay on the floor. "As I wished it twisted in my hands like a snake."

"Well, I don't see the money," said his son, as he picked it up and placed it on the table, "and I bet I never shall."

"It must have been your fancy, Father," said his wife, regarding him anxiously.

He shook his head. "Never mind, though; there's no harm done, but it gave me a shock all the same."

They sat down by the fire again while the two men finished their pipes. Outside, the wind was higher than ever, and the old man started nervously at the sound of a door banging upstairs. A silence unusual and depressing settled upon all three, which lasted until the old couple rose to retire for the night.

"I expect you'll find the cash tied up in a big bag in the middle of your bed," said Herbert, as he bade them good night, "and something horrible squatting up on top of the wardrobe watching you as you pocket your ill-gotten gains."

II

In the brightness of the wintry sun next morning as it streamed over the breakfast table, he laughed at his fears. There was an air of prosaic wholesomeness about the room which it had lacked on the previous night, and the dirty, shriveled little paw was pitched on the sideboard with a carelessness which betokened no great belief in its virtues.

"I suppose all old soldiers are the same," said Mrs. White. "The idea of our listening to such nonsense! How could wishes be granted in these days? And if they could, how could two hundred pounds hurt you, Father?"

"Might drop on his head from the sky," said the frivolous Herbert.

"Morris said the things happened so naturally," said his father, "that you might, if you so wished, attribute it to coincidence."

"Well, don't break into the money before I come back," said Herbert, as he rose from the table. "I'm afraid it'll turn you into a mean, avaricious man, and we shall have to disown you."

His mother laughed, and following him to the door, watched him down the road, and, returning to the breakfast table, was very happy at the expense of her husband's credulity. All of which did not prevent her from scurrying to the door at the postman's knock, nor prevent her from referring somewhat shortly to retired sergeant majors of bibulous habits when she found that the post brought a tailor's bill.

"Herbert will have some more of his funny remarks, I expect, when he comes home," she said, as they sat at dinner.

"I dare say," said Mr. White, pouring himself out some beer; "but for all that, the thing moved in my hand; that I'll swear to."

"You thought it did," said the old lady soothingly.

"I say it did," replied the other. "There was no thought about it; I had just—What's the matter?"

His wife made no reply. She was watching the mysterious movements of a man outside, who, peering in an undecided fashion at the house, appeared to be trying to make up his mind to enter. In mental connection with the two hundred pounds, she noticed that the stranger was well dressed and wore a silk hat of glossy newness. Three times he paused at the gate, and then walked on again. The fourth time he stood with his hand upon it, and then with sudden resolution flung it open and walked up the path. Mrs. White at the same moment placed her hands behind her, and hurriedly unfastening the strings of her apron, put that useful article of apparel beneath the cushion of her chair.

She brought the stranger, who seemed ill at ease, into the room. He gazed furtively at Mrs. White, and listened in a preoccupied fashion as the old lady apologized for the appearance of the room, and her husband's coat, a garment which he usually reserved for the garden. She then waited as patiently as her sex would permit for him to broach his business, but he was at first strangely silent.

"I—was asked to call," he said at last, and stooped and picked a piece of cotton from his trousers. "I come from Maw and Meggins."

The old lady started. "Is anything the matter?" she asked breathlessly. "Has anything happened to Herbert? What is it? What is it?"

Her husband interposed. "There, there, Mother," he said hastily. "Sit down, and don't jump to conclusions. You've not brought bad news, I'm sure, sir," and he eyed the other wistfully.

"I'm sorry—" began the visitor.

"Is he hurt?" demanded the mother.

The visitor bowed in assent. "Badly hurt," he said quietly, "but he is not in any pain."

"Oh, thank God!" said the old woman, clasping her hands. "Thank God for that! Thank—"

She broke off suddenly as the sinister meaning of the assurance dawned upon her and she saw the awful confirmation of her fears in the other's averted face. She caught her breath, and turning to her slower-witted husband, laid her trembling old hand upon his. There was a long silence.

"He was caught in the machinery," said the visitor at length, in a low voice.

"Caught in the machinery," repeated Mr. White, in a dazed fashion, "yes."

He sat staring blankly out at the window, and taking his wife's hand between his own, pressed it as he had been wont to do in their old courting days nearly forty years before.

"He was the only one left us," he said, turning gently to the visitor. "It is hard."

The other coughed, and rising, walked slowly to the window. "The firm wished me to convey their sincere sympathy with you in your great loss," he said, without looking round. "I beg that you will understand I am only their servant and merely obeying orders."

There was no reply; the old woman's face was white, her eyes staring, and her breath inaudible; on the husband's face was a look such as his friend the sergeant might have carried into his first action.

"I was to say that Maw and Meggins disclaim all responsibility," continued the other. "They admit no liability at all, but in consideration of your son's services they wish to present you with a certain sum as compensation."

Mr. White dropped his wife's hand, and rising to his feet, gazed with a look of horror at his visitor. His dry lips shaped the words, "How much?"

"Two hundred pounds," was the answer.

Unconscious of his wife's shriek, the old man smiled faintly, put out his hands like a sightless man, and dropped, a senseless heap, to the floor.

III

In the huge new cemetery, some two miles distant, the old people buried their dead, and came back to a house steeped in shadow and silence. It was all over so quickly that at first they could hardly realize it, and remained in a state of expectation, as though of something else to happen—something else which was to lighten this load, too heavy for old hearts to bear. But the days passed, and expectation gave place to resignation—the hopeless resignation of the old, sometimes miscalled apathy. Sometimes they hardly exchanged a word, for now they had nothing to talk about, and their days were long to weariness.

It was about a week after that that the old man, waking suddenly in the night, stretched out his hand and found himself alone. The room was in darkness, and the sound of subdued weeping came from the window. He raised himself in bed and listened.

"Come back," he said tenderly. "You will be cold."

"It is colder for my son," said the old woman, and wept afresh.

The sound of her sobs died away on his ears. The bed was warm, and his eyes heavy with sleep. He dozed fitfully, and then slept until a sudden cry from his wife awoke him with a start.

"The monkey's paw!" she cried wildly. "The monkey's paw!"

He started up in alarm. "Where? Where is it? What's the matter?"

She came stumbling across the room toward him. "I want it," she said quietly. "You've not destroyed it?"

"It's in the parlor, on the bracket," he replied, marveling. "Why?"

She cried and laughed together, and bending over, kissed his cheek.

"I only just thought of it," she said hysterically. "Why didn't I think of it before? Why didn't you think of it?"

"Think of what?" he questioned.

"The other two wishes," she replied rapidly. "We've only had one."

"Was not that enough?" he demanded fiercely.

"No," she cried triumphantly; "we'll have one more. Go down and get it quickly, and wish our boy alive again."

The man sat up in bed and flung the bedclothes from his quaking limbs. "Good God, you are mad!" he cried, aghast.

"Get it," she panted; "get it quickly, and wish—Oh, my boy, my boy!"

Her husband struck a match and lit the candle. "Get back to bed," he said unsteadily. "You don't know what you are saying."

"We had the first wish granted," said the old woman feverishly; "why not the second?"

"A coincidence," stammered the old man.

"Go and get it and wish," cried the old woman, and dragged him toward the door.

He went down in the darkness, and felt his way to the parlor, and then to the mantelpiece. The talisman was in its place, and a horrible fear that the unspoken wish might bring his mutilated son before him ere he could escape from the room seized upon him, and he caught his breath as he found that he had lost the direction of the door. His brow cold with sweat, he felt his way around the table, and groped along the wall until he found himself in the small passage with the unwholesome thing in his hand.

Even his wife's face seemed changed as he entered the room. It was white and expectant, and to his fears seemed to have an unusual look upon it. He was afraid of her.

"Wish!" she cried, in a strong voice.

"It is foolish and wicked," he faltered.

"Wish!" repeated his wife.

He raised his hand. "I wish my son alive again."

The talisman fell to the floor, and he regarded it shudderingly. Then he sank trembling into a chair as the old woman, with burning eyes, walked to the window and raised the blind.

He sat until he was chilled with the cold, glancing occasionally at the figure of the old woman peering through the window. The candle end, which had burnt below the rim of the china candlestick, was throwing pulsating shadows on the ceiling and walls, until, with a flicker larger than the rest, it expired. The old man, with an unspeakable sense of relief at the failure of the talisman, crept back to his bed, and a minute or two afterward the old woman came silently and apathetically beside him.

Neither spoke, but both lay silently listening to the ticking of the clock. A stair creaked, and a squeaky mouse scurried noisily through the wall. The darkness was oppressive, and after lying for some time screwing up his courage, the husband took the box of matches, and striking one, went downstairs for a candle.

At the foot of the stairs the match went out, and he paused to strike another, and at the same moment a knock, so quiet and stealthy as to be scarcely audible, sounded on the front door.

The matches fell from his hand. He stood motionless, his breath suspended until the knock was repeated. Then he turned and fled swiftly back to his room, and closed the door behind him. A third knock sounded through the house.

"What's that?" cried the old woman, starting up.

"A rat," said the old man, in shaking tones, "a rat. It passed me on the stairs."

His wife sat up in bed, listening. A loud knock resounded through the house.

"It's Herbert!" she screamed. "It's Herbert!"

She ran to the door, but her husband was before her, and catching her by the arm, held her tightly.

"What are you going to do?" he whispered hoarsely.

"It's my boy; it's Herbert!" she cried, struggling mechanically. "I forgot it was two miles away. What are you holding me for? Let go. I must open the door."

"For God's sake don't let it in," cried the old man, trembling.

"You're afraid of your own son," she cried, struggling. "Let me go. I'm coming, Herbert; I'm coming."

There was another knock, and another. The old woman with a sudden wrench broke free and ran from the room. Her husband followed to the landing, and called after her appealingly as she hurried downstairs.

21

He heard the chain rattle back and the bottom bolt drawn slowly and stiffly from the socket. Then the old woman's voice, strained and panting.

"The bolt," she cried loudly. "Come down. I can't reach it."

But her husband was on his hands and knees groping wildly on the floor in search of the paw. If he could only find it before the thing outside got in. A perfect fusillade of knocks reverberated through the house, and he heard the scraping of a chair as his wife put it down in the passage against the door. He heard the creaking of the bolt as it came slowly back, and at the same moment, he found the monkey's paw, and frantically breathed his third and last wish.

The knocking ceased suddenly, although the echoes of it were still in the house. He heard the chair drawn back and the door opened. A cold wind rushed up the staircase, and a long loud wail of disappointment and misery from his wife gave him courage to run down to her side, and then to the gate beyond. The street lamp flickering opposite shone on a quiet and deserted road.

A CLOSER LOOK

A classic example of an early 20th-century horror story, "The Monkey's Paw" first appeared in *Harper's Monthly* magazine in 1902 and was reprinted the same year in W. W. Jacobs's short-story collection, *The Lady of the Barge*. It was a hit with the public and critics alike, but strangely, Jacobs was best known at the time as a humorist whose favorite subject matter was the lives of sea captains and dockworkers; his foray into the macabre was almost a fluke.

Jacobs was most popular in an era that began to bridge the gap between Victorian and early 20th-century literature. During the time of Queen Victoria's rule in England (1837–1901), most of the world's literature could be described as being "Victorian" because it shared certain qualities and themes. Victorian novelists such as Charles Dickens popularized the tales of hardworking, virtuous characters who found happy endings, but by the late 1800s, many novelists had begun to take a decidedly more fantastic approach to literature. This perhaps reflected the influence of Gothic themes, which had been simmering in the background since the late 1700s but had been overtaken by the rise of Victorianism. With its combination of romance and horror, Gothic literature survived through the Victorian Age and entered the 20th century in the form of sensational writing often known as pulp fiction. Reading had become a popular pastime among the masses, as books were more readily available and affordable than ever before, and most people in the English-speaking world possessed at least a basic education. The public clamored for stories about anything it could get its hands on, from adventures on the high seas to detective stories, and a well-crafted tale of horror was sure to captivate a wide audience.

Perhaps as a holdover from the Victorian era, Jacobs's tale included an obvious moral lesson—be careful what you wish for—as well as dire consequences for disregarding the lesson. The moral of the story is most clearly stated in the fakir's intentions for the paw, as reported by the character of Sergeant Major Morris: "'He wanted to show that fate ruled people's lives, and that those who interfered with it did so to their sorrow'" (8). When people begin meddling in affairs that are better left to a higher power such as God or fate, the results can be disastrous and can create quite the opposite effect from what was intended.

While the point of the story may be Victorian, the gloomy atmosphere of the setting is reminiscent of Gothic literature, and it begins, ominously enough, on a cold and wet night. The White family's house is set on a lonely, forsaken road, and it seems an inhospitable place until the focus shifts to the warm family scene inside the house. The mood changes again once the family's visitor, Sergeant Major Morris, begins talking solemnly about the terrible magic of the monkey's paw. The family is entranced by the sergeant major's curious object, especially the young man Herbert, who, in the typical invincibility of youth, believes that nothing truly horrible could come of wishing on the paw. He encourages his father to try it, despite Morris's repeated warnings to the contrary, asserting that the wished-for sum of 200 pounds would enable his parents to "be quite happy" (11). His words will literally come back to haunt the Whites, as the stage is set for a Gothic ghost story to commence.

Like any good suspense author, Jacobs builds in instances of foreshadowing to subtly signal major events or turns in the plot. For example, while playing chess with his son, Mr. White is described as one who sees "a fatal mistake after it was too late" (5); after Mr. White wishes, Herbert remarks, "'Well, I don't see the money, . . . and I bet I never shall'" (12), and Mrs. White comments, "'how could two hundred pounds hurt you, Father?'" (13). Such words seem harmless at the time, but upon further review, the foreshadowing effects are plainly seen and take on greater significance. For it is only after Herbert's tragic accident at the factory that Mr. White realizes the "fatal mistake" he made in wishing for 200 pounds, and the Whites discover that such a sum could indeed harm them emotionally when offered as compensation for their dead son's life. As for Herbert, his bet was dead on; he never did see the money.

Although the shriveled monkey's paw is often described within the story as a "talisman," this object is not one that brings good luck. It has quite the opposite effect instead. After Mr. White's first wish, for 200 pounds, results in disaster, Mrs. White presses him to use the second to wish their son alive again. She unreservedly believes in its power now, but in the confusion of her grief, she asks for something unwise. Acting against his better judgment, Mr. White complies but then changes his mind and uses the third wish to send the supposedly undead Herbert away. With that, the magic and mischief of the paw expire, and the husband and wife are left in solitude once again. No longer an ominous setting, the "quiet and deserted road" represents relief from an untold horror, but it will remain a lonely place for the grieving parents.

ABOUT THE AUTHOR

William Wymark Jacobs (better known as W. W.) was born in London on September 8, 1863. Because his father was a dockworker on the River Thames, the family lived in an area of London called Wapping, which was close to the docks in the historic Port of London. Despite coming from a poor and large family, Jacobs received a private-school education, and at the age of 16, he began working as a civil service clerk in the Post Office Savings Bank. Six years later, in an effort to make some extra money, he published his first short story, but his was a long road to fame.

Jacobs's first collection of stories, *Many Cargoes*, was published in

W. W. Jacobs

1896, followed by a novel (*The Skipper's Wooing*) and another short-story collection (*Sea Urchins*), all of which combined to elevate his popularity among readers and increase his standing among fellow writers. Further guaranteeing his success was the deal Jacobs struck with *The Strand,* a monthly fiction magazine, to continuously run his stories and provide him with a steady income for almost as long as he lived. Jacobs joined the ranks of other prominent authors—such as Agatha Christie, Arthur Conan Doyle, and Somerset Maugham—also published in *The Strand.* During the 1890s and into the early 1900s, the magazine enjoyed a readership of about 500,000 people, which made it a successful jumping-off point for many authors' careers.

By 1899, Jacobs was able to leave his day job for one that he actually enjoyed—writing full-time. He married Agnes Eleanor Williams, who was most known for her involvement in the women's suffrage movement, in 1900 and set up a comfortable household north of London. The first of their five children was born in 1901, when Agnes was 20 years old and Jacobs was 38. The following year saw the publication of another Jacobs short novel, *At Sunwich Port,* as well as *The Lady of the Barge,* which included two horror stories, "The Monkey's Paw" and "The Toll-House." This experiment with the macabre became a huge success for Jacobs, and he continued to dabble in the horror genre.

However, Jacobs took the inspiration for the majority of his sto-

A dockworker tending a barge in the bustling Port of London

ries from his childhood memories of growing up near the busy docks and wharves and from his contemplative walks along the seaside later in life. His favorite characters were sailors and dockworkers, retired captains and officers, barmaids and nagging wives—a cast of people with whom he was quite familiar and uniquely able to bring to life on the page. Like such contemporaries as American authors O. Henry and Mark Twain, Jacobs used the vernacular of the lower-class dockland citizens to capture the essence of his characters and make them true to life.

Jacobs's last collection of short stories, *Night Watches*, appeared in 1914. By 1916, his production of stories and novels had slowed, and after that year, his output was next to nothing. He spent time converting several early works into short plays, preferring to recycle old material instead of creating new plots and characters. He had first adapted "The Ghost of Jerry Bundler" for the stage in 1899, which encouraged him to continue in this line of work. Jacobs's stories remained popular throughout the first three decades of the 20th century, and many early books continued to be reprinted as fiction readership regained strength after World War I ended in 1918.

Jacobs died just days before his 80th birthday in 1943, still one of the most prolific and popular authors of his time. However, his work fell into oblivion in the following years, and only certain stories, such as "The Monkey's Paw," were plucked out and revived as selections in anthologies. Today, the man who was known most for the strong output of humorous, satirical pieces during his lifetime is most recognized for the famous tale of the magical monkey's paw.

Published by Creative Education

P.O. Box 227, Mankato, Minnesota 56002

Creative Education is an imprint of The Creative Company.

www.thecreativecompany.us

Design by Rita Marshall; production by Christine Vanderbeek

Page 24–31 text by Kate Riggs

Printed by Corporate Graphics in the United States of America

Photographs by Alamy (David Baillie), Corbis (Christie's Images, Hulton-Deutsch

Collection), Getty Images (John Atkinson Grimshaw, Hulton Archive)

Cover and illustration page 2 © 2010 Etienne Delessert;

illustrations pages 22, 32 © 2010 Gary Kelley

Library of Congress Cataloging-in-Publication Data

Jacobs, W. W. (William Wymark), 1863–1943.

The monkey's paw / by W. W. Jacobs.

p. cm. — (Creative short stories)

Summary: A mummified monkey's paw carrying a spell grants three

wishes to each of its owners and fulfills them in unexpected and terrible

ways. Includes an analysis of the story and a biography of the author.

ISBN 978-1-58341-919-9

1. Wishes—Fiction. 2. Fate and fatalism—Fiction. 3. Horror stories. I. Title. II. Series.

PZ7.J15255Mo 2010   [Fic]—dc22   2009027888   CPSIA: 120109 PO1090

First edition

2 4 6 8 9 7 5 3 1